ISLAND BABY

BY HOLLY KELLER

A MULBERRY PAPERBACK BOOK   NEW YORK

Watercolor paints and a black pen were used for the full-color art.
The text type is Della Robbia Bold.

ISBN 0-688-13617-6

10 9 8 7 6 5 4 3 2

The Library of Congress has cataloged the
Greenwillow edition of *Island Baby* as follows:
Keller, Holly.
Island baby / by Holly Keller.
p.   cm.
Summary: Pops, a man who runs a bird hospital
on an island, and his young helper Simon nurse an
injured baby bird back to health.
[1. Birds—Fiction.   2. Wildlife rescue—Fiction.
3. Islands—Fiction.]   I. Title.
PZ7.K28132Is   1992
[E]—dc20   91-32491   CIP   AC

FOR BARRY

Pops poured a mug of juice for Simon and
one for himself. Then they sat on the front steps
without talking and watched the sea.
Simon wriggled his toes.
"It's hot," he said.
"Yup," Pops agreed, "and time to get to work."

Simon set down his mug and went into the old
shack. The screen door banged shut behind him.
A parrot on a perch near the roof began
to squawk.
Simon looked up and smiled. "I'm coming," he said.
Then he filled the red can with seeds and the silver
one with fruit, the way Pops had shown him.

Everybody on the island knew about Pops's bird hospital. Sometimes he had so many sick birds to take care of, the noise made Simon's head ache. But he loved Pops's birds, and he came to help him every morning.

"You're going to be a fine bird doctor," Pops had told him, and Simon liked to think about having his own bird hospital some day.

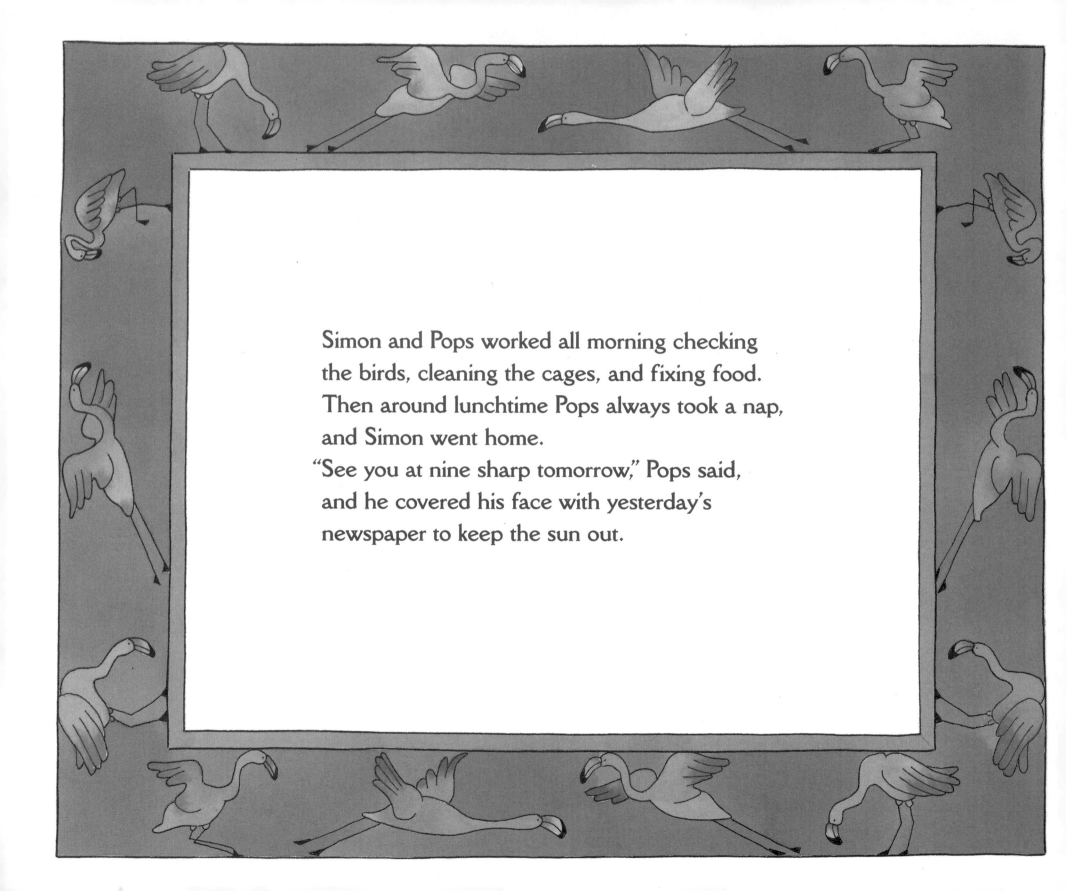

Simon and Pops worked all morning checking
the birds, cleaning the cages, and fixing food.
Then around lunchtime Pops always took a nap,
and Simon went home.
"See you at nine sharp tomorrow," Pops said,
and he covered his face with yesterday's
newspaper to keep the sun out.

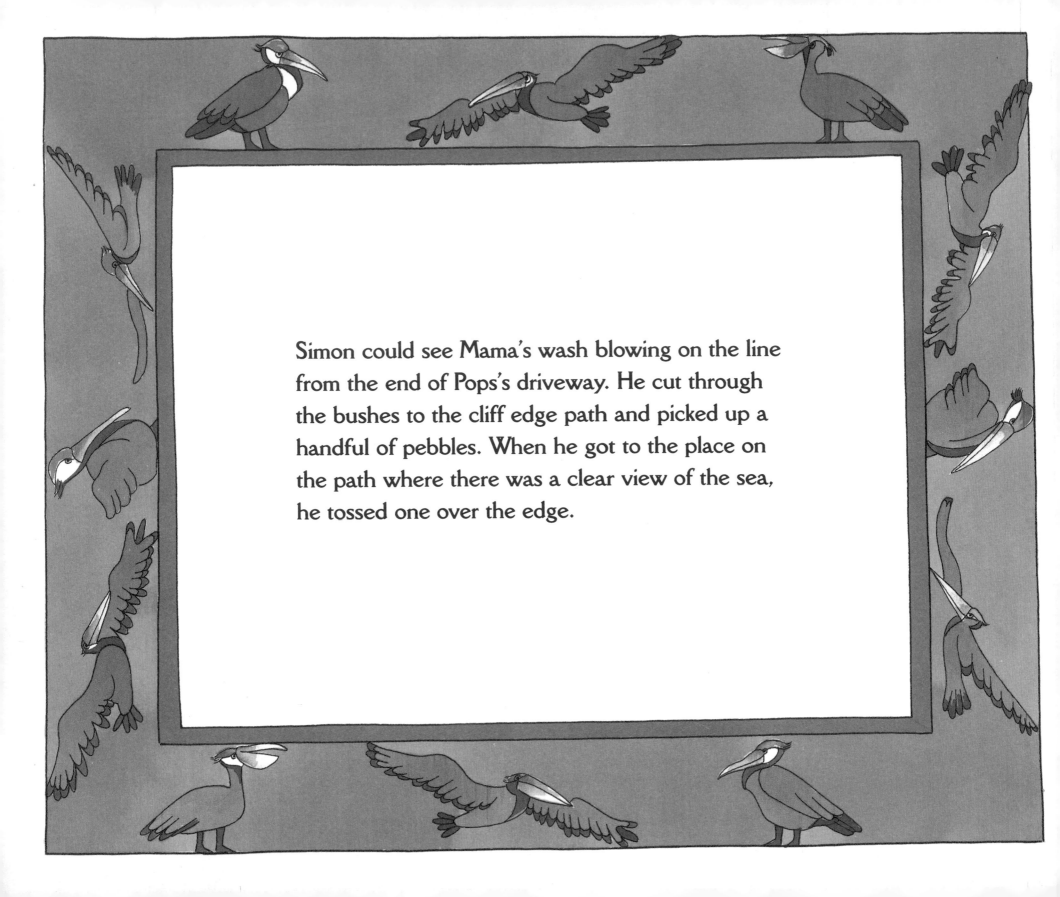

Simon could see Mama's wash blowing on the line
from the end of Pops's driveway. He cut through
the bushes to the cliff edge path and picked up a
handful of pebbles. When he got to the place on
the path where there was a clear view of the sea,
he tossed one over the edge.

Simon looked down to see where it had landed. A small bird was bobbing up and down in the water. He watched as the bird was pulled out by the sea and then hurled back in against the rocky cliff wall, over and over again.

"Fly," Simon yelled. "Why don't you fly away?"

But the bird didn't move.

Simon skidded down the gravelly cliff until he stood
ankle deep in the swirling foam. The rocks were
slippery, and each time he tried to grab the bird, the
water pulled it away.

It was a long time before he realized that Pops was
standing behind him. Pops had a net, and in a few
minutes the baby flamingo was in it.

"One of his legs is broken," Pops said, "and he's pretty
banged up."

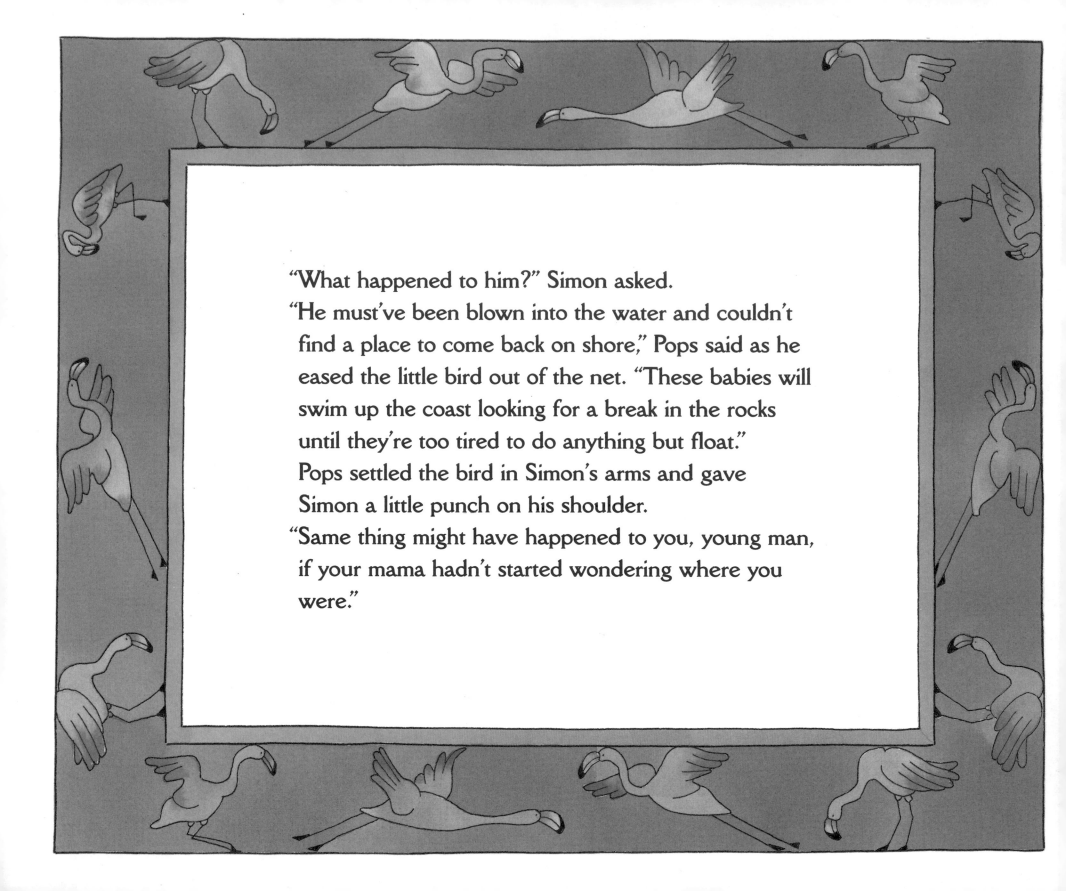

"What happened to him?" Simon asked.

"He must've been blown into the water and couldn't
find a place to come back on shore," Pops said as he
eased the little bird out of the net. "These babies will
swim up the coast looking for a break in the rocks
until they're too tired to do anything but float."

Pops settled the bird in Simon's arms and gave
Simon a little punch on his shoulder.

"Same thing might have happened to you, young man,
if your mama hadn't started wondering where you
were."

Simon went back to the hospital with Pops and
helped bandage the bird's leg. They put him in an
empty cage, and Pops wrote the date on the
clipboard he kept hanging on a nail.
"What do you want to call him?" Pops asked.
Simon shrugged. "I don't know," he said. "Why not
just Baby?"
And Pops wrote that down, too.

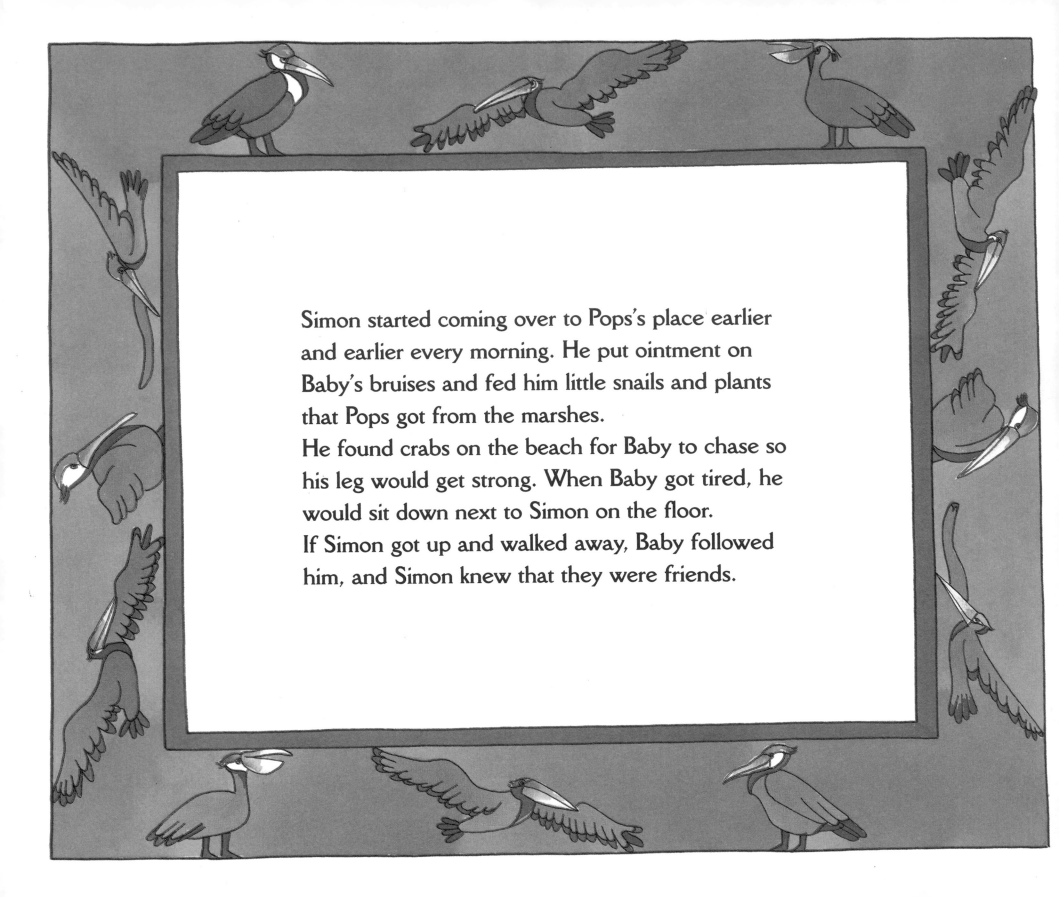

Simon started coming over to Pops's place earlier and earlier every morning. He put ointment on Baby's bruises and fed him little snails and plants that Pops got from the marshes.

He found crabs on the beach for Baby to chase so his leg would get strong. When Baby got tired, he would sit down next to Simon on the floor.

If Simon got up and walked away, Baby followed him, and Simon knew that they were friends.

Baby's leg was healed by the end of the summer,
and Pops said the words that Simon had been
dreading.

"I think it's about time to set Baby free."

"I don't want to," Simon said, and he rested his
cheek on Baby's soft back.

Pops pulled on his beard and shook his head.

"Now, that would be a fine thing, wouldn't it?"
he said. "You'd be going off to start school,
and I'd be left here to care for this spoiled baby
of yours."

Simon knew Pops was joking, but he didn't laugh.
The next morning Pops was waiting for Simon in
the truck. Simon got Baby and climbed up onto
the front seat.

It took about twenty minutes to get to the big salt
marsh at the end of the island, and Simon couldn't
think of anything to talk about.

"Just wade in with him a bit and set him down,"
Pops said when he turned off the motor.

Simon was quiet when he got back to the truck,
and Pops concentrated on his driving.
"He looked okay," Simon said finally, when they were
almost home, "but I still wish he could have stayed."
Pops nodded.

After dinner Simon helped Mama take the wash
off the line. A cloud of bright pink flamingos
raced across the sky.
"Baby will be up there soon," he told Mama,
feeling suddenly proud.
"You did a good job," she said.

"Mama," Simon asked, "when I start going to school, will you miss me?"

"Of course I will," Mama said, "but I'll be proud of you, too."

And they walked toward the house together.